Through The

Every Reflection Hides A Lie

AARON

To Lily, With Love!

Contents

Prologue – Through the Dark Glass

The first time I saw Lily, the world betrayed me.

One moment I was another consultant and analyst in another gray conference room, choking down lukewarm coffee and waiting for the project kickoff to end. The next, the air had changed. Heavier. Charged. The kind of shift you feel in your bones before a storm breaks.

I didn't hear her name at first, I only saw her eyes. Wide, steady, luminous. They caught me like a hook catches flesh. Something in my chest snapped tight. A connection. No, that word was too small. This was recognition. Ancient, inexplicable. A tether stretching across lives, lifetimes, centuries maybe, pulling me toward her whether I wanted it or not.

The conference room blurred. Laughter, introductions, the shuffle of paper gone. My pulse thundered in my ears.

Then her hand slipped into mine. Warm. Familiar. Too familiar. My brain whispered *you've touched her before*. I don't know when, I don't know where, but the certainty burned in me like fire under skin. For those few seconds, I wasn't myself anymore. Something inside me broke open, raw and exposed.

And then it was gone.

I let her hand go, dazed, only half-aware that another man, a colleague, was waiting impatiently for his handshake. I'd made a fool of myself, staring too long, forgetting basic manners. I didn't care.

I sat down again, trembling, and one verse echoed in my head, the way a bell echoes long after its struck:

For now, we see through a glass, darkly; but then face to face.

That day, I saw her face.

And I knew with a clarity that chilled me, I had just met my flame, my mirror, and my undoing.

Part One: Obsession

Chapter 1 – The Spark

Two days later, the fire hadn't dimmed.

I woke with her face in my dreams. I saw her eyes in the dark glass of my laptop screen. Even in meetings, while colleagues droned on about upcoming testing deadlines and risk reports, I replayed that moment again and again: her hand in mine, the heat, the recognition.

I told myself it was nothing. A crush. A harmless distraction. But by the time I caught myself typing her name into search engines, scouring public records, scrolling through social networks, I knew I was lying.

Her name alone haunted me: **Lily Ann Bradshaw**. Soft syllables, unusual, unforgettable. It first appeared as a CC line on a project email, then as a voice on weekly calls, guiding us through reports. That voice, melodic, deliberate, a little sing-song, turned dry data into music.

At the roundtable lunch, she'd been magnetic. I remembered John, the treasury manager, teasing her about being named after a flower. She didn't flinch. She just explained, calm and precise, that "Lily" came from North Carolina's state wildflower. One line, and the table full of men went silent.

And then she kept talking. Dressage competitions. A career in geology. A chemical company merger where she'd joked, she'd been "congratulated on retirement" while still young. Her colleagues laughed. I didn't. I was too busy listening to her voice, each word sinking under my skin.

That night, I found her pictures. Running in college, smiling on a horse, laughing with friends at an amusement park. Each image lit me up and hollowed me out at the same time. I couldn't stop.

Then I found the detail that stopped me cold: she was married. With a child.

For a few minutes I couldn't breathe. My screen blurred. The floor seemed to drop out from under me. I should have stopped there. Closed the browser. Let her go.

But instead, I remembered her eyes, and the fire surged back, fiercer than before. How could something that felt so destined be wrong?

I told myself I just wanted to be her friend. That friendship was innocent, safe, enough. But the truth gnawed at me: I didn't want friendship. I wanted *everything*.

Every day at work, while colleagues praised my diligence and my boss AJ dropped by with his questions, I was searching for her. Not just online. In every face, every name, every accidental reminder. A road named Bradshaw Farms. A colleague named Carol Ann. It was all her. Always her. I was tripping, I knew it. But obsession, once lit, doesn't ask for permission. It just burns.

And somewhere deep inside, a darker thought whispered: if destiny had delivered her to me, maybe rules no longer mattered.

Chapter 2 – Cracks in the Glass

The project went live that week. On paper, it was flawless.

Files moved. Reports balanced. The bank's systems processed transactions. My manager AJ slapped my back and said I'd saved the day. But the only thing I cared about was whether Lily would be on the go-live call.

She wasn't.

Her colleague Michelle handled everything with her usual military precision clipped voice, emotionless greetings, efficient to the point of cruelty. The call was a success, but for me, it was hollow. I'd come for one reason: to hear Lily's voice again.

That night, as background jobs ran and the system spat out transfer files, I sat alone in the office and opened my browser. *Soulmates. Inyun or Inyeon. Karmic relationships. Past-life connections.* The search results blurred together. Some sites claimed a soulmate always meant joy. Others warned that karmic ties could lead to ruin.

I leaned back in my chair, eyes burning, and whispered to the empty cubicle:

"So which one are you, Lily? My salvation or my destruction?"

The next morning, my inbox answered. A flood of error reports had landed. The bank's systems couldn't process certain special characters. Files were being rejected. Urgent. Critical. Fix immediately.

For anyone else, it would have been a nightmare. For me, it was a gift. Because every rejection meant more emails. Every fix meant calls. Every failure meant Lily.

And soon, we were talking every day.

She sounded different outside the group calls. Warmer. More human. When I apologized for the errors, she reassured me with a line I replayed until the words lost meaning: *"It's great to work with a client that's so proactive."*

My chest tightened reading it. Proactive. Professional. Harmless. She had no idea what those words did to me.

But cracks were forming. In me. In her. In the glass between us.

Because then came John.

I ran into him in the corridor one afternoon, his face red with irritation. He'd just hung up the phone and muttered, "Can you believe it? I had to call Lily incompetent. She deducted fees without approval."

My pulse spiked. He'd humiliated her. Wounded her. I felt the blow as if it had been aimed at me. That night, I wrote her an email, not technical, not professional, but personal.

No one deserves to be spoken to like that. You've always been diligent, prompt, and professional. I respect you more than you know.

It was reckless. Crossing the line. But it worked.

Her reply was soft, almost grateful: *We can only do our best and move on when things like this happen.*

The ice was broken.

And in the weeks that followed, the emails multiplied. Friendly. Personal. A photograph of her with her horse. Stories about her childhood. Admissions she never voiced in meetings.

I sent pictures too, me at the Cherry Blossom Festival, me holding work trophies. Pathetic, maybe. But it felt like we were weaving a secret thread between us, line by line.

Except she never gave me her personal number. Never accepted my Facebook request.

Once, when I called her desk after hours, hoping just to hear her voicemail, she picked up. Her voice was gentle, but her words cut deep: *"I don't do personal talk during office hours or after."*

I apologized. Too many times. She forgave me, in that careful way people forgive when they want distance. But then, one evening, she accepted my LinkedIn invitation. A small concession. Enough to feed the fire.

I told myself friendship was enough. That I could live on scraps of connection. But late at night, when my inbox stayed silent, I knew it was a lie.

And that lie was rotting me from the inside.

Chapter 3 – The Itch

Obsession is a hunger. Feed it, and it grows. Starve it, and it consumes you anyway.

By the third week, the silence returned. Her replies became clipped. Busy. Always busy. *"Super busy around here! Hoping it will die down soon." "Over 2000 emails waiting for me!" "Vacation coming up, lots to prepare!"*

I stared at her words and felt my chest tighten with a pain I'd never known. Was this heartbreak? Or withdrawal?

The emptiness was unbearable. I ate chocolate until my stomach hurt. Drank until I couldn't think. I gained ten pounds in days. None of it dulled the ache.

At night I dreamed of her eyes. In the morning, I woke with tears already on my face. Every road sign, every stray word reminded me of her. Bradshaw Farms. Carol Ann Drive. Even coincidences became wounds.

And then one night, I felt something new. Not love. Not longing. Something sharper.

An itch.

A desperate need not just to see her, not just to hear her, but to bind her to me. To become necessary. Indispensable.

Because if I couldn't keep her attention through affection… maybe I could keep it through need.

That thought, the first seed of something dark took root.

And once it did, there was no going back.

Chapter 4 – Friendly Fire

The system never really settled. Even after go-live, small errors kept bubbling up: a misplaced decimal here, a duplicate transfer there. Each problem meant more emails, more excuses to reach out, more reasons for her to respond.

I told myself it was frustrating. But deep down, I was grateful for every glitch.

Her messages had changed. At first, they were stiff, all numbers and policy jargon. Now, she slipped in fragments of herself, almost like she'd forgotten she was talking to a stranger.

"Sorry for the delay, had to drop my son at daycare."
"Can you resend the file? My horse trainer texted right as I hit save and I lost focus."
"Mother-in-law's visiting this weekend, so trying to get ahead of the workload."

Ordinary details. Innocent. To her, they were nothing. To me, they were everything. Proof that I was inside her orbit, closer than the others who only saw her polished surface.

One afternoon, she attached a screenshot of a corrected report. At the bottom, she'd signed her name without the usual formalities: no *Regards*, no *Thanks*. Just,

Lily.

That single word nearly undid me.

I stared at it for hours, tracing each letter, imagining her typing it in a rush, unaware of the power it held. My mind twisted it into a secret signal, a private intimacy meant only for me.

I replied immediately. Too eagerly. Too many exclamation points. I reread it ten times before hitting send button, but the damage was done. My desperation bled through the screen.

When her reply came back, brief and businesslike, I panicked. Had I pushed too far? Had I scared her?

That night, I couldn't sleep. I lay in bed rehearsing explanations, excuses, half-truths. If she pulled back, I'd tell her I was just friendly. Just tired. Just professional. Anything to keep the thread from snapping.

Because by then, the thread was everything.

In the office, my colleagues started to notice. AJ stopped by my desk, leaning on the partition with that managerial smile of his.

"You're buried in something," he said. "Hope it's not more Bradshaw errors."

I forced a laugh, minimizing her email. "Just keeping the lights on."

He nodded, satisfied, and walked away. He didn't see the truth. No one did. To them, I was the diligent consultant, the reliable problem-solver.

But behind the screen, I was chasing every word she gave me like a starving man chasing crumbs.

Friendly fire, I told myself. That's all it was. Harmless little sparks between emails.

But I knew better.

I wasn't being burned by stray sparks. I was already in the fire.

Chapter 5 – The Gift of Silence

It started with a gap.

One day without a reply. Then two. Then three.

I told myself she was busy. Her inbox is overflowing. Her son must be needing attention. Her horse, her husband, her life, all of it tugging her away. I repeated the excuses like a prayer, but prayers don't quieten the hunger.

I refreshed my inbox until my eyes blurred. Each empty minute felt like rejection. Each passing hour, like a verdict. By the second day, I had memorized the pattern of her absence: no green light beside her name, no quick notes with emojis tucked at the end, no unexpected midnight replies that proved I was on her mind too.

It was silence. A cold, perfect silence.

I lasted until the third day before breaking.

"Hey, Lily, just checking if you saw my last note. Totally understand if you're swamped."

I deleted it. Too eager. Too obvious.

"Let me know when you're free, no rush at all."

Deleted again. Weak. Groveling.

Finally, I forced myself to wait, to hold the line. To prove to myself I could endure. But the waiting hollowed me out.

I tried to fill the void. Chocolate. Whiskey. Streaming shows I couldn't follow. None of it worked. At night, I dreamed of her eyes, luminous and untouchable, staring at me from across a gulf I couldn't cross. I woke up with tears on my face, my body heavy with grief for something I hadn't even lost yet.

By the fourth day, I cracked.

I pulled one of her photos from my saved folder, the one of her smiling at the amusement park, hair windblown, laughter frozen in pixels. I printed it and pinned it inside my desk drawer, hidden from everyone else. Each time I opened the drawer, I felt closer. Each glance was a shot of oxygen in drowning lungs.

Finally, on the fifth day, her name appeared in my inbox again.

"Sorry for the late reply, things have been crazy here. My son's got a cold; work is piling up. Hope you're doing well."

I read it once. Twice. Ten times. Every word a salve, every mundane detail a gift.

Her son had a cold. She'd chosen to tell me that. Not AJ. Not Michelle. Me.

I leaned back in my chair, dizzy with relief, and whispered to the empty office: "You came back. I knew you'd come back."

It didn't matter that it was just a polite excuse, the kind people sent without thinking. To me, it was proof. Proof she hadn't forgotten. Proof she still saw me.

And that night, for the first time in days, I slept.

But the silence had left a scar. I realized something I hadn't before:

Her presence lit me on fire. Her absence hollowed me out.

And one day, when the silence returned, I might not survive it.

Chapter 6 – Crossed Wires

The joke should have been harmless.

It was one of those casual roundtable lunches the bank insisted on, where mid-level managers rubbed elbows with consultants like me, all of us pretending the cafeteria food was palatable. AJ was there, laughing too loud. John sat at the end, stirring his soup like it had personally offended him.

Then Michelle leaned in with that sly little smirk she reserved for colleagues she didn't quite respect.

"So, how's *LAB* doing these days? Lily Ann Bradshaw, LAB. She runs like a science experiment."

The table chuckled. A few more quips followed. Something about her "mothering tone" on calls. Someone imitated her voice.

And I felt my blood boil.

Before I knew it, I was leaning forward, voice sharper than it had any right to be. "You know, maybe you should respect the person who catches your errors before the clients do. Half the reason your numbers balance at all is because of her."

Silence. Utter silence. Forks froze halfway to mouths. Eyes darted from me to each other.

John raised an eyebrow. "Easy, Aaron. It was a joke."

I forced a smile, but it felt like my face might crack. "Right. A joke. Just don't forget who's holding the team together."

The conversation limped on, but I could feel the shift. A subtle edge of discomfort clung to me, as if I'd revealed too much.

Later that afternoon, my inbox pinged. Her name.

"You didn't have to defend me, but… thank you."

Seven words. That was all.

But I read them like scripture. Over and over. Parsing the pause before the thank you. Imagining the softness in her voice as she typed it.

She *noticed*. She knew I'd stood up for her. She was grateful.

The others could laugh, could sneer, could pretend she was just another name on a spreadsheet. But she wasn't. Not to me. And now, maybe, not to her either.

That night, I dreamed of her again. But this time it wasn't her eyes haunting me. It was her voice, low and warm, whispering my name across the dark.

When I woke, heart hammering, I didn't feel ashamed.

I felt chosen.

Chapter 7 – The First Betrayal

I should have stopped digging.

It started innocently enough, another late-night search, another round of names and addresses. I told myself it was professional curiosity, background knowledge, risk mitigation. Lies. Every keystroke was hunger.

And then I found him.

Her husband. A bland headshot on a corporate site. Beige tie, thinner smile, the kind of man who disappears in a crowd. A LinkedIn profile full of dull jargon: operations, metrics, quarterly projections. He looked like paperwork which had come to life.

But it wasn't his job that gutted me. It was the mortgage records. The property taxes. Their tidy little house with its tidy little family history. Proof that he lived in her world in a way I never could. Proof that every glance she gave me, every message, every shared laugh, belonged to someone else first.

I sat staring at the screen, pulse pounding, bile rising in my throat. My hands shook.

Married. With a child.

The words clanged in my skull like iron bars slamming shut.

She had told me, of course. Casually, like it was nothing. *"My husband's picking up our son tonight."* A line dropped in the middle of a call, tossed away like small talk. I had smiled at the receiver, made some polite reply, and no one else noticed.

But inside, I was shattering.

It wasn't jealousy. It was betrayal.

I'd felt it in my chest like a knife sliding between ribs. She had stood before me that first day, hand in mine, eyes binding me in fire, and somehow she hadn't thought to mention there was already a ring on her finger? That she had a life I could never touch?

The screen blurred. My vision tunneled.

I opened a new email draft and stared at the blank page.

He doesn't know you the way I do.
He doesn't see you the way I see you.
You don't belong with him.

The words poured out, a confession and a manifesto, raw and violent in their need. My fingers hovered over the Send button. For one wild moment, I wanted to unleash it all, to force her to see, to make her admit what she must have known since the first handshake.

But I didn't.

I sat frozen, sweat dripping, until finally I saved the draft and slammed the laptop shut.

The words remained, unsent but alive, a ghost crouched in my outbox.

And as I lay in bed that night, staring at the ceiling, I realized something with terrifying clarity:

I could not undo what had begun.

Her marriage wasn't a boundary. It was a wound.

And wounds demand to be fed.

Chapter 8 – Fire and Ash

It wasn't enough anymore.

The emails, the polite thanks, the rare glimpses into her life, they had fed me once. Fed me like crumbs feed a starving man. But now they tasted of ash.

I wanted more.

She sent me pictures once. Not of herself, not really, just her horse, a dressage competition ribbon, a blurred snapshot from a geology field trip years ago. Innocent images. Harmless.

But I studied them as if they were scripture. I zoomed in on her smile, memorized the curve of her jaw, the stray hair that slipped free of its clip. I traced the shape of her house in the background, noted the model of her car, the color of the siding. Details. Anchors. Proof that she existed beyond the screen.

I answered in kind, sending her photos of my own life. The cherry blossoms in spring. My work trophies lined up like a shrine. A curated version of myself, someone worth noticing. Someone worthy of her.

Her replies were polite. *"Beautiful trees."* *"Congrats on the awards."* Nothing more.

Each word felt like a droplet of water on a tongue cracked from thirst. For a second, relief. Then only the ache again.

And worse: silence grew between the drops.

I refreshed my inbox compulsively. Opened old emails just to reread her words. Her voice lived in my head like a haunting, her laugh echoing in dreams that left me waking in tears.

But the more I consumed, the emptier I became.

One night, drunk and furious with myself, I pulled up the photo of her at the amusement park again. Wind in her hair, laughter frozen in pixels. I stared until my eyes burned. Then I whispered into the empty room:

"You don't belong with him. You belong with me."

The words hung in the dark, dangerous and undeniable.

For the first time, I didn't feel ashamed.

I felt entitled.

Her absence gnawed at me, carved me out. Her presence, even in fragments, lit me on fire. I was burning at both ends, fire and ash.

And I knew, with certainty, that chilled and thrilled me in equal measure:

I couldn't keep living on scraps.

Sooner or later, I would need more.

Part Two: The Scheme

Chapter 9 – Necessary

Need is cleaner than love.
It doesn't argue. It doesn't moralize. It simply arrives and takes a seat at the head of the table.

I decided to make myself necessary.

It started small, so small I could still lie to myself about it. The nightly report queue would choke on a character it had always choked on; the retry job I wrote would run, but I would schedule it to *notify me* instead of resolving automatically. A hiccup. Nothing more. Just enough to force a human hand. Just enough to require *my* hand.

When the alert pinged, I waited. One minute. Three. Five. The internal channel lit up with routine chatter. Then her name appeared in my inbox.

"Seeing rejects on the 10:15 batch, can you take a quick look? Sorry to bug you at this hour." , L

Bug me. The phrase wrapped around my ribs like a ribbon. I replied in sixty seconds that felt like a ceremony.

"On it."

A call followed. Her voice was tired, the late-night softness that made it feel like she was sitting right beside me.

"I hate to ask," she said. "But I don't want this to roll into morning."

"You never have to apologize to me," I said. "This is what I'm here for."

That night, the "fix" was a single switch in a place no one else would think to look. I toggled it. The batch cleared. She exhaled, relieved. Gratitude poured through the line like warmth.

"You're a lifesaver, Aaron."

Lifesaver. Necessary. I slept like a saint and woke like a sinner.

After that, the pattern found me. An index that needed rebuilding would just happen to wait for her shift; a scheduled job would graze the edge of her deadline window until she messaged, *Can you jump on for me?* I didn't break anything, I told myself that often, as if repetition could bless the act. I only *withheld inevitabilities* for a beat, and only long enough that she learned the same lesson I had, when something mattered, **she needed me**.

On Thursday, AJ stopped by my desk.

"You're glued to their queue," he said, smiling in a way that measured. "I appreciate the hustle. Just make sure you don't become a single point of failure."

"I won't," I lied.

When he left, I stared at my own reflection in the black corner of my monitor. A dark glass, a darker version of me looking back. I lifted my hand and the shadow lifted his. Necessary, we mouthed to each other.

Weeks like this teach you a new calendar. Not Monday through Sunday, but *When She Writes* and *When She Doesn't*. On a day she wrote, my blood was bright. On a day she didn't, the world felt like a warehouse full of dead light.

By the end of the month, Lily's emails had changed color. They were still professional, still careful, but you can hear reliance even when it's dressed in formality. She had started to ask me first. Not the team. Not Michelle. Me.

"Quick gut-check, if the totals swing again, can I route to you first?"
"If you're online later, I'd love your eyes on a discrepancy."
"You always see the pattern faster."

Always. The word hit like sacrament.

One night, close to midnight, she called without emailing first. The line clicked and I heard only her breath for a second, wind across a phone, an empty kitchen, the quiet that wraps a house when a child finally sleeps.

"Are you free?" Her voice was hushed.

"For you? Yes."

A pause. "You're too kind."

No. Not kind. Strategic. But I didn't say that. I guided her through a check, the kind of little dance we'd invented together: review the summary, compare the deltas, flatten the noise until the pattern appeared. While we worked, her guard slipped. She told me her son had learned to say a new word that day. She laughed softly as she repeated it, as if afraid to wake a door.

When the numbers reconciled, she whispered, "I don't know what I'd do without you."

There it was. The sentence I'd been engineering, spoken like a secret. I let it sit on my chest and burn a careful hole.

"I'm glad I can help," I said. "You deserve less chaos."

A beat. "Thank you, Aaron. For... being there."

After we hung up, I stayed in the dark office, staring at the city's scattered lights. Somewhere, people were touching each other without fear. I touched the cool edge of my desk and pretended her hand was there, just beyond the glass of the screen. I didn't need touch. Not yet. I needed the sentence to live inside her: **Without him, this breaks**.

The next afternoon, Michelle cornered me at the coffee machine, her smile the kind that doesn't reach her eyes.

"You and Lily are quite the late-night duo," she said lightly. "We see the status pings."

"We work well," I said.

She stirred her coffee. "We all work well. But it shouldn't *depend* on one person."

"You're right," I said, meaning *you're too late*. "It shouldn't."

Michelle let the silence hang, as if waiting for me to blink. I didn't. She walked away, heels tapping, and I realized something else had shifted: this wasn't only about Lily anymore. Making myself necessary to *her* was making me dangerous to everyone else.

That night, I looked through my saved emails, all the small proofs that we were becoming a private mechanism: her thanks, her midnight *are you there?*, her *I'd love your eyes.* I collected them like talismans. My hands shook. Not with fear. With hunger.

I opened a new draft, her name auto filled so fast it felt like fate.

When the totals swing, don't escalate to the whole chain. Route to me first. I can buffer the noise.
Delete. Too direct.

If this keeps happening, we can build a smaller review path. Just you and me.
Delete. Too obvious.

I finally typed: *There's a cleaner way to handle the nightly drift. No need to wake the world for it. Happy to discuss when you're free.*
Send.

Fifteen minutes later:

"Appreciated. Tomorrow 4:30?"

I stared at those three words as if they were coordinates. Tomorrow, 4:30. A private meeting. A room without Michelle's eyes or AJ's laughter. A door I could close behind us. I imagined the shape of the whiteboard. The way she'd stand, arms folded, listening. The way she'd say my name when something clicked. The way 'need' would thicken the air between us like humidity before a storm.

The next day, the conference room was colder than I'd imagined, the projector too bright. She arrived with a notebook and that disciplined smile that makes men underestimate her. I had printed diagrams. I had highlighted risks. I spoke carefully, balancing truth and omission like plates on a stick.

"Right now," I said, "any out-of-tolerance movement wakes the entire chain. It creates noise. People jump in and clog the lane. If we narrow the triggers and set a single checkpoint, we cut the panic by eighty percent."

Her pen moved, quick. "And the checkpoint?"

I met her eyes for one long second. "Me. For now."

She didn't flinch. She considered, nodded once, then again, slower. Her trust landed between us with a soft sound.

"Okay," she said. "For now."

Two words. A hinge swinging open. I felt the hidden machinery of the room tilt.

We spent an hour adjusting thresholds, trimming alerts, shaping a smaller corridor the data would travel before it ever reached daylight. None of it broke policy. None of it set off alarms. It merely rearranged the pathways so that one person, *I*, stood where the sirens used to be. A human baffle. A necessary gate.

When we finished, she closed her notebook and smiled with something like relief. "This will help," she said. "It'll help a lot."

"I'm glad," I said. "You don't need the noise."

She hesitated, then added, "I don't need the noise. I need results."

The sentence glowed. Results. I was no longer a favor. I was a function.

We walked out together. Michelle passed us in the hall and looked between our faces like they were clues in a puzzle she didn't like. Lily told her, crisp and measured, "We're slimming the alert path. Aaron will be first pass for a while."

"For a while," Michelle repeated. She wore a smile that promised an audit later. Let her audit.

By then, the pattern would be habit; habits are the softest chains.

That night, before the 10:15 batch, I stood by the window and watched the last smear of pink drain from the sky. The city clicked into its nocturnal grammar: lights; sirens; the far river sounding like air going in and out of a sleeping chest. I thought of Lily's voice in the dark kitchen, of the way my name sounded when she needed it. My hands felt steady. Too steady. The kind of steadiness you only get when you've convinced yourself the worst thing is also the right thing.

At 10:16, an alert whispered through the new corridor. A small drift. Harmless. It walked straight to me and stopped there, obedient. No one else knew. No one else had to.

I cleared it. The system purred.

A minute later, my phone lit up.

"Saw your update. Thank you."

I typed *Always* and deleted it. I typed *Anytime* and deleted that too. I settled on: *Of course.*

Of course I will stand at your gate. Of course I will shoulder your storms. Of course, I will build the path that makes me indispensable and then pretend I just happened to be standing there when the road was laid.

Because love had failed me.
Because silence had nearly killed me.
Because need asks fewer questions.

I put the phone down and looked at my reflection in the glass again. The city behind me. The dark version of me in front. I touched the window and for a split second the cold made it feel like I was touching his hand.

"Necessary," I whispered.

He nodded back.

Chapter 10 – The Leak

Patterns have a sound.
Once you've tuned your ear to them, you hear what others don't.

By mid-March, the system sang to me. Tiny fluctuations in totals, harmless drifts in reconciliation, double–posted reversals that would cancel themselves by the next day. No one else noticed. Or if they did, they shrugged them off as noise.

I didn't.

Noise is a curtain. Behind it, sometimes, are doors.

At first, I did what I'd always done, fixed the blips before daylight. It made me indispensable. It kept Lily reaching for me first. But one night, looking at a string of nearly identical variances, a new thought arrived, soft and treacherous:

What if the two of us *owned* the curtain?

I didn't call it theft. Not then. I called it "better control." "Reducing noise." "Single point of truth." Words that let me keep one foot in the light.

The next time I talked to Lily, I seeded the idea like a test.

"You know," I said, sharing my screen, "half of these rejects are just reversals. The system flags them anyway and it creates panic. If we held them in a quiet queue before releasing, we could prevent a ton of false alarms."

She tilted her head, scanning the columns. "Held them where?"

"A staging bucket. One only we see. We'd just...filter first."

"Is that normal?" she asked.

"Efficient," I said. "The normal process is wasteful."

Her lips pressed together. She didn't say yes. She didn't say no. She just said, "Show me."

I showed her. Not the whole thing, just enough to make it look like common sense. She nodded, wrote notes. When she left, she thanked me. I heard no suspicion in her voice, only relief.

Relief is a foothold. Once someone feels it, they want it again.

I began building the "quiet queue" that night. A simple script. No alarms. No tickets. Transactions paused there for review, my review, before surfacing to the system. All perfectly reversible. All invisible to anyone who didn't know where to look.

I didn't break policy; I rearranged it. I didn't steal; I staged. These were the lies I whispered to myself.

The first week it ran, Lily sent me a message at 11:47 p.m.:

"The reports look so much cleaner. Is this the new logic?"

I typed, *"Yes. Less noise, more signal."*
Deleted it.
Typed, *"Exactly. Just a test for now."*
Send.

Her reply came back:

"Good. This will save me headaches."

Save her headaches. Save her time. Save her. I was the quiet hero behind the curtain, holding back the storm.

The second week, she began routing anomalies to me directly, no CC to Michelle or AJ. Just a subject line: *Need your eyes first.* She didn't even ask where they went after.

The third week, she asked a question I had been waiting for:

"Should we tell anyone about the staging bucket?"

I stared at the words, my pulse quicker. This was the moment. If she truly didn't know, this was her chance to say *this isn't allowed*. If she did know but wanted to keep it quiet, she was already stepping through the door.

I typed back:

"Not yet. Let's make sure it works. No need to confuse them with details." Send.

A pause. Then:

"Okay. Not yet."

Two words. A hinge swinging shut.

That night, I couldn't sleep. The glow from the monitor painted the room like a confession booth. The queue ticked quietly in the background, transactions pausing, waiting, obeying. Lily's name at the top of my inbox felt like a seal on a pact she didn't even know she'd signed.

I told myself it was still harmless.
I told myself I was still fixing.
I told myself she needed me.

But deep down, in the quiet just before dawn, I understood what had begun.

There was a leak now.
And we were standing on the wrong side of it together.

Chapter 11 – Unsent No More

For weeks, I lived with unsent drafts. Half-confessions, half-manifestos. Pages that bled *her* name again and again.

You're the only one who sees me.
I think about you when I close my eyes.
He doesn't deserve you.

Lines I wrote at two in the morning, hands trembling, then erased by dawn when the sun made them look mad.

But silence is a weight. The longer you carry it, the heavier it grows. Eventually, it crushes you, or you drop it on someone else.

One Tuesday night, after another round of "quiet queue" staging, I opened a new message and began typing, slow, deliberate, every word like threading a needle through my own skin.

Lily,

I've been meaning to tell you something, but I don't want you to take it the wrong way. You're the only person in this project I actually trust. When everything else feels chaotic, I know I can rely on you. You're the reason the numbers balance, the reason anyone sleeps at night. Please don't share this, I just needed you to know.

It wasn't romantic. Not exactly. It wasn't professional either. It was the gray middle space where true danger lives: intimate enough to pierce, vague enough to deny.

I hovered over *Send*. My chest pounded. My reflection in the dark monitor glass leaned in, eyes hungry.

Do it.

Click.

For five minutes, I couldn't breathe. I convinced myself I'd crossed a line she would recoil from, that I'd detonated everything.

Then my phone buzzed.

"Thank you. That means a lot. Some days it feels like no one notices. I appreciate you saying it."

Seven sentences. Each one a fuse burning deeper into me.

She hadn't run. She hadn't scolded. She hadn't closed the door. She'd let it stand. She'd even admitted something back: *some days it feels like no one notices.*

No one notices. Except me.

That night, I didn't sleep. I sat at my desk with her reply open, rereading every word, analyzing every pause, every softened phrase. The more I stared, the more it transformed. It wasn't just gratitude, it was confession. Proof of a private thread binding us.

The next day, I tested the water again. A smaller draft.

Sometimes I feel like we're the only two who really see the cracks. Everyone else is blind, but we keep the whole thing upright. Just you and me.

I deleted it. Too obvious. Wrote another.

Glad you're on this project. I'd be lost without you.
Send.

Her reply:

"Likewise. It helps knowing someone else is keeping watch."

Keeping watch. The phrase sank its claws into me. She'd given me a role, a title. Not consultant. Not analyst. *Watcher.* The one who sees for her.

That evening, when I closed the queue alone, I whispered into the empty office:
"You don't know it yet, Lily, but you just opened the door."

The unsent drafts were unsent no more.

And there would be no closing that door again.

Chapter 12 – A Dangerous Dance

Every conspiracy starts with a convenience. A shortcut. A harmless little workaround that no one intends to weaponize.

That's what I told myself, anyway.

The first time it happened, it was almost too small to matter. A misaligned total on the Tuesday batch. I'd seen it building for days, a duplication that would cancel itself if left alone. Normally I would have fixed it quietly, the way I always did. But that night, instead of intercepting it early, I let it slip just far enough that she noticed.

Her email arrived within twenty minutes.

"Totals aren't reconciling, can you look?"

The words sent a jolt through me. Not because of the problem. Because of the *we*. Her problem was now ours.

I called instead of replying. Her voice was tight, on edge.

"End of day balances have to tie," she said. "If this doesn't resolve, John will have my head."

"Don't worry," I said. "I've got you."

I walked her through the "solution", a correction I'd already prepared, disguised as a rescue. She followed my instructions line by line; her relief audible when the totals snapped back into place.

"You're a miracle worker," she said.

"No," I corrected softly. "We just know where to look."

We. Always we.

The next day, I seeded another test. A false discrepancy, subtle enough to pass as system noise. By evening, she'd flagged it. By night, she was on the phone with me again, the sound of typing in the background, her breath uneven.

"This is insane," she muttered. "Half the time I don't know if I'm catching errors or chasing shadows."

"You're catching them," I said. "Because you've got me."

She laughed, exhausted. "Sometimes I wonder if it's us holding the bank together."

My throat tightened. *Us.* She'd said it herself this time.

After we hung up, I sat staring at the ceiling of my apartment. The air felt different, heavy with implication. She might not have realized what she was admitting, but I did: we had crossed from colleagues into co-conspirators, even if she didn't name it that way.

The third time, it was deliberate. I engineered a small transaction shift, a harmless drift between internal ledgers. Nothing criminal, not yet. Just enough to trigger her instinct. She pinged me instantly.

"Flagged something strange again, need your eyes."

I replied: *"Don't escalate yet. Let's keep this between us until, we're sure."*

There was a pause before her reply. Long enough for me to imagine her frowning, hesitating, considering the weight of my words.

Then her answer:

"Okay. Between us."

Between us.

I whispered the phrase aloud, savoring it. It wasn't just collusion; it was intimacy dressed in the language of secrecy.

That night, I lingered on the call longer than necessary after we resolved the variance. She didn't hang up right away either. The silence between us stretched, not awkward but charged, like we were waiting for someone else to say the thing we both pretended not to know.

Finally, she said, "I should go."

"Of course," I replied.

But when the line clicked dead, I smiled. Because she hadn't said *I need to go.* She'd said *I should.* Obligation, not desire. Duty, not choice.

And in that difference, I heard the dangerous music of a dance just beginning.

Chapter 13 – First Blood

The first cut is always small.
A paper-thin slice across the system's skin, so narrow no one notices the blood.

I'd been preparing for weeks, laying the scaffolding, whispering reassurance to myself that I wasn't crossing lines, only managing "noise." But lines don't stay still. They shift, blur, dissolve. And one night, the line dissolved completely.

It began with a duplicate transfer, a routine hiccup. Normally I'd intercept and reverse one entry. This time, I let them both linger. Two payments scheduled for the same vendor, one legitimate, one waiting like a ghost in the quiet queue.

Lily pinged me, predictable as breath.

"Totals off again. Looks like duplication."

I replied, calmly. *"I see it. Don't escalate yet. I'll reconcile."*

She hesitated. Then:

"Okay. Between us."

That phrase, 'between us', was the oxygen I needed.

I rerouted the ghost. Instead of reversing, I shifted it through a shell account I'd mapped weeks earlier. A corridor carved inside the labyrinth, labeled innocently, masked by the same logic we'd "tested" together.

To the system, it was just another correction. To Lily, it looked like I had cleaned the mess. To me, it was something else entirely.

The first theft.

Tiny. Invisible. No one watching would call it anything but a fix. But I knew better. And once I pressed Enter, I felt it, heat rushing through my veins, faster than desire, sharper than whiskey. Terror and triumph braided together.

When the ledgers balanced, Lily's relief poured through the line:

"You're incredible. I don't know how you do it."

My hands shook. "Just pattern recognition."

She laughed softly. "Well, don't go anywhere. I need you."

Need. The word stabbed deep. This wasn't love. It wasn't even friendship. It was dependency, and dependency was stronger than either.

After we ended the call, I sat in the dark, staring at the transaction log. My reflection in the monitor looked like a stranger: eyes wide, lips curved in a smile that didn't feel human.

I whispered to him, to the shadow-me in the glass: "We did it."

He smiled back.

Somewhere across town, Lily slept peacefully, unaware that her name was now inked on the first page of a ledger she'd never meant to sign.

And me? I knew one truth more dangerous than any secret queue or midnight call.

The first cut is the hardest.
The second comes easier.
And the third, by then, you don't even feel the blade.

Chapter 14 – Shadows in the Ledger

The morning after the first transfer, I walked into the office as if nothing had changed. AJ was joking with Michelle about her new shoes. John was muttering about exchange rates. Normal. Routine. The kind of banality that makes people blind.

But I knew everything had changed.
I carried a secret no one else could see, except Lily.

At least, I told myself she saw it.

The duplicate payment was gone from the ledgers, balanced like it had never existed. No red flags, no alarms. But in my chest, alarms screamed with a fevered ecstasy: we had done something no one else could undo.

That evening, Lily's message arrived.

"Totals look clean today. Appreciate you staying on top of it."

Clean. She said clean. She didn't ask how, didn't want the details. She accepted the gift and moved on.

I read it repeatedly. Some part of her had to know. She wasn't stupid. She was the sharpest mind in that building. Maybe she didn't want to name it. Maybe she wanted to believe in the magic of clean numbers, delivered by me.

And so, I gave her more magic.

Each week, a new "correction." Tiny. Unremarkable. Sometimes a shifted decimal, sometimes a duplicate routed away, sometimes a balance trimmed to perfection. Each time, I wrapped it in the language of reassurance.

"Handled before daylight."
"Noise suppressed, nothing to worry about."
"We're good, always."

And each time, she replied with gratitude that I soaked into my bones.

I knew what I was doing. I was tightening the knot. Not only did she need me, she also trusted me with her blind spots. Every correction was another thread binding her fate to mine.

But threads become ropes. Ropes become nooses.

And one night, staring at the queue, I wondered: was I tying us together? Or tying her down?

Chapter 15 – The Mirror Game

The drafts on my computer grew bolder. No longer half-confessions, but strategies. Scripts for conversations that hadn't happened yet. Notes for responses I wished she'd sent.

I began saving them in a hidden folder called *Mirror*. Because that's what it felt like: every message from her reflected back to me through the dark glass of my obsession, warped until it looked like what I wanted.

When she wrote: *"Thanks for catching that."* I saw, *'I need you more than anyone.'*

When she wrote: *"Busy week ahead, might be offline."* I saw, *'I'll miss you.'*

The mirror never showed me her truth. Only mine.

One night, emboldened by the clean run of another staged correction, I slipped again.

Lily, I typed. *Sometimes it feels like it's just us against the system. If anyone else knew how much you carry, they'd crumble. I hope you know how much I admire that strength.*

This one I almost didn't send. It was too close to naked. Too close to worship.

But my finger clicked *Send* anyway.

Her reply came later that night, short but not dismissive:

"You're kind. Don't put me on a pedestal, I'm just doing my job."

A rejection, on the surface. But the mirror twisted it. *Don't put me on a pedestal* meant she knew she was already on one. *Just doing my job* meant she recognized I was watching more than the job.

I let the mirror feed me until my head spun.

The next day, I engineered another correction, slightly larger, still invisible, a few thousand skimming the edge. Harmless, I told myself. Nothing she'd question.

And when she thanked me again, the mirror showed me the only truth I wanted to see:

We weren't just colleagues.
We weren't just conspirators.
We were partners.

In work. In secrecy. In crime. In us.

Chapter 16 – Lines in the Sand

Numbers stop meaning what they used to once you cross them often enough.

At first, I told myself it was just a few thousand pennies lost in the churn of a multinational bank. Then a few thousand became ten. Ten became fifty. By the time the totals flickered into six figures, I no longer flinched.

Because numbers weren't money anymore. They were proof. Proof that the system trusted me. Proof that Lily trusted me.

Every time she clicked "approve," I imagined it wasn't just a transaction. It was a vow. A whispered *yes* across the glass.

She never asked questions. That was the part that thrilled me most. She saw anomalies. I "corrected" them. She signed off. She didn't want details, didn't demand explanations. Maybe she was too tired, too overworked, too grateful to have someone else carrying the burden. Or maybe, just maybe, she knew more than she let on.

That thought kept me alive at night: that she knew and chose me anyway.

One Friday evening, the discrepancy was larger than usual, a swing of eighty-four thousand, masked behind a vendor split I'd engineered. I sent her the sanitized ledger, neat and reconciled. She replied within minutes:

"Thank you, Aaron. This could've been ugly".

I stared at that line for a long time. *Could've been ugly.* Not *was.* Not *how did you fix it?* Just quiet gratitude, wrapped in trust.

I typed back: *"I won't let ugly reach you."* Deleted it.
Typed: *"Happy to help."*
Send button pressed.

But the mirror twisted it into the message I really meant, '*I am your shield. You're mine now.*'

Over the next week, I pushed harder. Slightly larger shifts timed so she'd be the one to see them. Every time, she routed them to me without looping in Michelle, without even copying AJ. Her silence was complicity, whether she realized it or not.

And still, no questions.

No questions is an answer. It means keep going.

Michelle caught me once by the coffee machine, eyeing the dark circles under my eyes. "You look like hell. Are you carrying too much for them?"

I smiled. "I don't mind. Someone has to."

She frowned, as if trying to read something hidden in my face. But she never saw it, the lines I'd already crossed, the sand already behind me.

That night, I sat alone in the glow of the staging bucket, the numbers shifting like shadows. For the first time, I wasn't nervous. I wasn't hesitant. I was calm, steady, sure.

This wasn't a line anymore. This was the new ground I stood on.

And once you redraw the sand, you stop looking back at where it used to be.

Chapter 17 – The Web Tightens

Michelle had a talent for sniffing out rot. Not because she was brilliant, she wasn't, but because suspicion was her default setting. She assumed everyone was sloppy, everyone was lazy, everyone was hiding something. And most of the time, she was right.

So, when she started asking questions, I knew the net was tightening.

It began with an off-hand comment in a status meeting.

"Funny how all the anomalies seem to route to Aaron first," she said, stirring her tea like it was no big deal. "Almost like the system knows who its favorite is."

The room chuckled politely. AJ gave me a wink; the kind bosses give when their star employee gets ribbed. But I caught the flicker in Michelle's eyes: this wasn't a joke. It was a probe.

That afternoon, she emailed Lily directly:

"Can you clarify why Aaron's the first checkpoint for reconciliations? Thought protocol was to escalate through treasury review."

I saw it in the shared chain before Lily answered. My pulse hammered. This was the moment it could all unravel.

Lily's reply was measured, diplomatic.

"Aaron's been extremely proactive. With him screening, fewer unnecessary alarms reach the broader group. We'll revert if needed, but for now this reduces noise."

For now.
That phrase again. My phrase. Our phrase.

Michelle didn't push back right away, but I could feel her circling. She started popping into late-night calls she had never joined before. She lingered in chat threads that used to be quiet. She was watching.

So, I gave her something to watch.

The next week, I seeded a false error, just sloppy enough that it would look like *her* oversight if she touched it. When Lily routed it to me, I "fixed" it and sent a note up the chain.

"Caught a misalignment in treasury's staging. Flagged and resolved."

The phrasing was careful: not an accusation, just an implication. AJ skimmed it, nodded, moved on. But Michelle noticed. Her lips pressed thin the next time I saw her. She didn't say anything, but silence can carry as much venom as words.

Later that evening, Lily messaged me privately.

"Thank you for catching that. She's been breathing down my neck lately. Good to have backup."

Backup. That's what she called me. The word blazed like a medal pinned to my chest.

She didn't realize what I'd done. Or maybe she did, and she accepted it, because I was on her side. Either way, Michelle was on the outside now. Outnumbered. Outmaneuvered.

That night, staring at the glass of my monitor, I felt the web tightening. Not around me. Around *us.*

Michelle was the spider on the edge, probing, suspicious. But Lily and I? We were already bound together in silk threads spun of secrecy and trust. She was tangled with me now. Even if she didn't want to be.

And webs don't unravel easily, they strangle.

Chapter 18 – The Point of No Return

There's a difference between theft and destiny. At least, that's what I told myself.

By the time the chance arrived, I was no longer trembling at the thought of another "correction." I was calm, methodical, almost reverent. The staging bucket hummed like an altar. All I had to do was lay the offering down.

It began with a vendor remittance, routine, boring, six figures spread across multiple accounts. I'd seen the structure a dozen times before. That night, I carved a sliver from the flow and redirected it through the ghost corridor I'd perfected, masked beneath layers of reconciliations. Not sloppy. Not obvious. Flawless.

When the system ran, it balanced. No alarms. No flags. Just smooth, clean totals.

Then came the keystroke.
Lily's.

She approved the ledger. One click. Casual. Thoughtless. A thousand approvals before, a thousand after. But to me, it was different.

That single keystroke felt like a vow. A ring slipped on my finger through the glass. Proof we were bound now, not just in secrecy, not just in late-night calls, but in crime.

I leaned back in my chair, heart pounding, watching the confirmation blink across the screen. In the reflection of the monitor, my face split into a grin I barely recognized.

"You said yes," I whispered.

Of course, she hadn't. Not in words. Not even in intention. But intention didn't matter anymore. The ledger was stamped. The money was gone. And her approval lived forever in the audit trail, binding her fate to mine.

Later that night, she sent a message, mundane, ordinary.

"Glad we got that one cleared. Would've been messy."

Messy. She had no idea how messy it already was.

I typed back: *"We make a good team."*
Send.

Her reply came quickly:

"Yes. We do."

Yes. That was all I needed.

I poured myself a drink, staring at the dark window of my apartment. The city lights scattered across the glass like a constellation, and in the reflection, the shadow-version of me raised his glass too.

"To us," I said. "No turning back."

He smiled. I smiled. We were married now, bound not by love or vows but by the ledger.

And the ledger never forgets.

Part Three: The Collapse

Chapter 19 – Fractures

Obsession is like glass under pressure.
At first it holds. Then the hairline cracks
appear. Tiny, invisible, but growing with every
breath.

The cracks began with silence.

Her emails, once quick, almost playful in their
brevity, were shrinking. *Thanks. Noted.
Handled.* One-word replies where once there
had been sentences. And the timing had
changed too. No more midnight messages. No
more sudden calls in the quiet hours when the
world belonged to us. Now her name appeared
only during the day, tucked between a hundred
others, stripped of intimacy.

I told myself it was the workload. Her son. Her
husband. Life. But deep down, I knew she was
pulling away.

I fought back in small ways. Crafted more
elegant fixes. Polished the numbers until they
shone. Slipped in lines that begged for
recognition: *"Handled this before anyone else
noticed." "Glad to take the heat for you."* But
her gratitude dulled. Her words became
generic.

And then came the worst: she started copying Michelle again.

Not always. Not on everything. But once or twice a week, her notes bore that extra pair of eyes. My chest tightened each time I saw the CC. It was betrayal in three keystrokes.

Michelle never replied directly, but I could feel her circling, the spider at the edge of the web. Watching. Waiting.

One evening, desperate, I called Lily directly. It rang too long before she picked up, her voice soft, distracted.

"Hi, Aaron. Can we make it quick? I'm just sitting down to dinner."

Dinner. With them. With him.

"I just wanted to be sure the variance was clear," I said, heart racing. "You saw the correction?"

A pause. Then, coolly: "Yes. Thank you. That's all fine."

Not *you're incredible*. Not *what would I do without you?* Just *thank you.*

I tried to prolong it. "I just, sometimes I feel like you don't realize how much I do to keep you protected."

Her silence was long. Too long. Finally, she said, carefully: "Aaron, I appreciate your work. But let's keep things professional, okay?"

The line went dead after that.

Professional.
The word echoed in my skull like a verdict.

I sat in the dark, staring at the reflection in the glass. The shadow-me looked cracked too, hairline fractures running through his face. I pressed my hand to the cold surface and whispered, "She doesn't mean it. She's afraid. She needs you. She'll come back."

But even as I spoke, the truth settled in my bones.

The glass was breaking.
And once glass breaks, it doesn't heal.

Chapter 20 – The Audit

Auditors never strike with one blow. They chip. They circle. They keep editing until the pattern beneath the edits reveals itself.

The second file hadn't rattled me. Not much. Questions are easy to answer if you control the language. But then the *third* file arrived, and that one felt different.

This time, they hadn't just asked for explanations. They had *edited my work*.

In the attached spreadsheet, my annotations had been crossed out, replaced by red comments in the margin:

- *"Standard filter does not apply to this transaction class. Please justify exception."*

- *"Staging bucket not documented in official procedures, provide change control record."*

- *"AR listed as both preparer and reviewer, independence compromised."*

Independence compromised. The phrase made my skin crawl. They weren't just circling anymore. They were cutting straight at the artery.

I stayed in the office long after midnight, rewriting their edits as if I could overwrite reality itself.

- *"Exception approved verbally by treasury manager, documentation pending."*
- *"Staging bucket was pilot control, temporary in scope. Validated by reduction in false alarms."*
- *"Reviewed with daily summaries; oversight maintained."*

Polished. Plausible. But it's thinner than paper. If anyone pressed, the lies would split open.

The next morning, Compliance didn't thank me for my annotations. They sent back a fresh file, this time with *highlighted cells*. Yellow for anomalies. Orange for repeat adjustments. Red for anything that tied directly to my ID.

The sheet glowed like a wound.

And this time, Lily's initials appeared too. Her approvals, stamped beside mine.

I stared at the red blocks next to her name until my vision blurred. To them, it meant exposure. To me, it meant binding. Proof she was tethered to me in ink no one could erase.

That night, she messaged me.

"They're digging deep. I'm nervous. Should we loop in AJ?"

Loop in AJ. The words sliced me open. Loop in AJ meant letting someone else between us. Loop in AJ meant losing the intimacy of secrecy.

I typed: *"If we involve AJ, the auditors will assume something's wrong. Better to keep it contained, cleaner that way."*
Send.

She replied minutes later:

"You're right. Let's contain it."

We. Us. Together.

But I knew better. This wasn't containment. This was a slow bleed. Every spreadsheet was a scalpel carving closer to the heart of what we'd built.

And no matter how many times I rewrote their edits, I couldn't stop the glass from cracking.

Chapter 21 – The Tipping Point

It was supposed to be another cut in the ledger's skin. Thin. Harmless. Clean. But greed dulls precision, and obsession clouds judgment.

The transaction landed in the staging bucket just before midnight, a quarterly vendor disbursement, high-volume, high value. Too tempting. I could have let it pass untouched. I could have kept the wound small. Instead, I carved deep.

Two hundred and fifty thousand dollars diverted through the ghost corridor. Not a sliver. Not a rounding error. A quarter million.

For the first time, the system flinched.

The totals balanced, but the timestamps lagged. The reconciliations hesitated a fraction longer than usual. And in the morning, the auditors pounced.

Their spreadsheet arrived with *red cells already filled in*.

- *"Material variance exceeds threshold. Please provide supporting documentation."*

- *"Transaction flow routed outside treasury path. Critical, explain exception."*

- *"AR identified as sole reviewer. Independence violation."*

Critical. The word blinked at me like a siren.

I rewrote their edits furiously. *Pilot control. Exceptions approved verbally. Validated against summaries.* Lies on lies, stacked like scaffolding around a collapsing building.

But this time, Lily noticed.

Her message came at 8:17 a.m., clipped, efficient.

"Aaron, auditors are pressing hard. Should we escalate to AJ? This amount is larger than usual."

My heart seized. She'd said *larger than usual.* She'd noticed the size. She hadn't asked where it went, hadn't demanded an explanation. She'd simply acknowledged it was unusual and then deferred to me.

I typed back: *"Escalating now would draw attention. Better to let me align the narrative before AJ sees it."*
Send.

Her reply: *"Okay. Just…be careful."*

Be careful. It was caution, maybe even distance. But the mirror twisted it into intimacy. *She's scared. She needs you to protect her.*

So, I did.

I scrubbed the logs, altered the batch timestamps, fabricated a duplicate anomaly to disguise the ghost transfer. I buried the evidence beneath layers of noise. And by morning, the totals looked clean again.

But the auditors weren't fools. They sent a new note, terse and sharp:

"Pending escalation to Audit Committee. Please be available for follow-up review."

The Audit Committee. The words were a death sentence.

Yet when Lily forwarded me the message, her comment was small, almost weary:

"Can you draft a response? I don't have the bandwidth for this."

I stared at the screen, breathless. She had given me her voice. Her authority. Her name.

And in that moment, I convinced myself of the only truth I could bear:

She knew. She knew and she was letting me speak for us.

We were partners. In secrecy. In fraud. In destiny.

Even if, in reality, she was just tired.

Even if, in reality, the glass was already shattering.

Chapter 22 – The Breaking Glass

The summons came in the form of a calendar invite.

No warning, no polite explanation, just a subject line in all caps: **FOLLOW-UP REVIEW: VARIANCE INVESTIGATION.**

It wasn't a meeting. It was a trial.

When I arrived, the room was already staged like an interrogation. A rectangular table. Laptops open. Compliance officers on one side, AJ at the head, his face unreadable. Michelle sat near the back, arms folded, eyes sharp and hungry.

Lily was there too.

She avoided my gaze as I sat down. Her hands were folded tightly in her lap, white at the knuckles. I wanted to reach across the table, touch them, whisper that it would be fine. But the glass between us had never been thicker.

The auditors began with edits, projected on the screen. Not spreadsheets this time, slides. Pages of red circles and highlighted cells. My initials flashing like warning lights.

- "Adjustment routed via AR queue without secondary review."

- "Staging bucket undocumented; violates control protocol."
- "Material variance of $250,000 concealed with fabricated duplicate."

Fabricated. They had used the word. The blade was in my chest.

AJ's voice was calm but clipped. "Aaron, they're saying these weren't just corrections. They're saying these were deliberate manipulations. I want to hear your explanation."

My throat tightened. Words crawled like insects. "System noise. Inefficiencies. I contained them before they escalated. That's why totals are always balanced. That's why no one lost money."

Michelle snorted. "No one lost money? A quarter million routed through a shadow bucket isn't noise."

I turned toward Lily, desperate. "Tell them. Tell them we agreed it was the best way to manage anomalies. You saw the improvements."

Her eyes flicked to mine, just for a second, then back down to her lap. Her voice was low, flat. "I...don't remember agreeing to that."

It was the sound of glass breaking.

A pall of silence fell. The auditors scribbled. AJ's frown deepened. Michelle's smirk widened. And me? I felt the floor tilt.

They asked more questions, but I don't remember the details. Dates, times, approvals. All I heard was Lily's sentence echoing through my skull: *I don't remember.*

Not denial. Not outright betrayal. But absence. A void where solidarity used to be.

By the end, the auditors closed their laptops with clinical finality. One of them said, "We'll be escalating to the Audit Committee."

Michelle looked satisfied. AJ looked tired. Lily looked like she wanted to disappear.

And me? I sat staring at my reflection on the black screen of the idle projector. Cracks ran through the shadow's face, jagged lines splitting the glass.

For weeks, I'd told myself she was with me. That her silence was consent, her approvals vows, her trust a tether.

But now the tether was cut. The glass was shattered.

And all that was left was the sound of it
breaking, repeatedly in my head.

Chapter 23 – The Betrayal

There are only two kinds of silence: the kind that comforts, and the kind that kills.

Lily's silence killed.

After the review meeting, she barely spoke to me. No late-night pings. No small acknowledgments. Days passed with nothing but clipped, daylight-only messages.

"Please review."
"Send me the totals."
"Forward to Compliance."

Each word stripped of softness, drained of gratitude. I told myself she was just frightened. That the auditors had spooked her, that she was pulling back to protect herself. But protection felt like rejection, and rejection cut deeper than any audit note.

Then came the worst blow.

She forwarded me an email from Compliance.

"Lily, please confirm your role in approving March 27 adjustment. Did you review supporting documentation or rely on AR's notes?"

Her message above it was short.

"Draft a reply for me."

Not *help me*. Not *what should I say?* Draft it. Like a secretary handing dictation to a clerk.

I wrote the reply anyway. My fingers trembled as I typed the lie that would shield us both:

"Reviewed totals, no anomalies noted. Relied on AR for technical reconciliation. Confirmed alignment before approval."

She sent it exactly as I wrote. No edits. No questions. No gratitude.

When I read her forwarded copy, I felt both triumph and fury. She had trusted me to put words in her mouth. That was the proof of our bond, wasn't it? But she hadn't thanked me. Not even a smiley, not even a *thanks*.

And in that absence, a whisper crept in, she was distancing herself so she could betray me.

That night, I couldn't stand the silence. I called her cell. Twice. No answer. The third time, she picked up, her voice low, tired.

"Aaron, it's late."

"I just wanted to hear you say it."

"Say what?"

"That you're still with me."

A pause, then: "I'm…handling this the best I can. Please don't make it harder."

Don't make it harder. The words scalded. To her, I was the problem now. The burden.

"You wouldn't even have survived this without me," I hissed.

"Aaron," She stopped herself, voice breaking. "I can't do this. Goodnight."

The line went dead.

I sat staring at the glass of my monitor, my reflection fractured into jagged shards. The betrayal was complete. She was cutting herself free of me, handing me to the auditors, letting me drown alone.

But she didn't understand. You can't betray what's already bound.

We were in this together, inked into the ledger, written in approvals, sealed by her keystrokes.

And if she wouldn't say yes willingly anymore, then I would force her hand.

Chapter 24 – Ashes

Ash doesn't burn. It only remembers.

The collapse began quietly. No sirens, no drama. Just another email in my inbox:

Subject: Audit Committee Review – Immediate Response Required
From: Compliance Office

I opened it with hands that already knew the truth.

They had traced the transfers. Not all, never all, but enough. The ghost corridor, once invisible, now lay outlined in their red edits. Each diversion tied back to my ID. Each approval stamped with Lily's initials, circled like evidence.

They summoned us separately. Lily went first. I waited in the hallway, palms sweating, heart hammering against my ribs. When she emerged, her face was pale, her lips pressed into a single hard line. She didn't look at me. Didn't even flinch when I whispered her name. She just walked past, eyes fixed on the exit.

Inside, the room was colder. The auditors asked questions I'd already rehearsed lies for, but this time their eyes told me the lies weren't working.

"Why were transactions rerouted?"
"Why was access limited to you alone?"
"Why did approvals lack supporting documentation?"

And always: "Did Lily know?"

I answered the only way I could. "Of course she knew. She approved everything. She relied on me, yes, but she was there. We were partners."

They scribbled notes. No nods, no reactions. Just the scratching of pens, like nails dragging across my skull.

Hours later, they dismissed me. No verdict, no sentence. Just silence.

But silence can kill.

That night, I walked past Lily's office. Empty. Stripped. Her nameplate gone from the door. It was as if she had never been there.

I tried calling. Once. Twice. A dozen times. Each time, the same mechanical voice: *"This number is no longer in service."*

She hadn't just betrayed me. She had erased me. Cut me out of her world like a tumor. Left me holding the rot alone.

The next morning, AJ met me with Security. No words, just an escort to collect my things. Michelle stood at her desk, watching, her face had unreadable expressions. Triumph? Pity? I couldn't tell.

At home, in the dark, I sat before the black mirror of my monitor. No queues. No reports. No Lily. Only my reflection, jagged with cracks that spread each time I blinked.

I pressed my hand to the cold glass and whispered her name.

"Lily."

No answer. Just ash where fire used to be.

Because fire consumes. It dazzles, it blinds, it burns everything in its path. And when it's done, nothing remains but gray dust and the memory of heat.

I thought I'd built a bond, a ledger that tied us forever. But all I'd built was fire.

Now I lived in ash.

Part Four: The Reckoning

Chapter 25 – The Cell

The walls weren't bars.
They were beige.
Beige paint, beige floor, beige ceiling. A box without color, built not to punish but to erase.

They called it "administrative detention." Not jail. Not yet. Just a holding place while Compliance finished their review and prosecutors sharpened their knives. But four beige walls feel the same whether you're awaiting trial or serving a sentence.

The cell had a table bolted to the floor, two chairs, and a camera in the corner with its little red eye blinking. The first time I noticed the camera, I waved. The shadow-me in the glass lens waved back.

They asked questions in cycles. Different faces, different suits, but always the same cadence.

"Why were the transactions rerouted?"
"Did anyone instruct you to create the staging bucket?"
"Was Lily aware of what you were doing?"

Lily. Always Lily. Her name repeated so often it became a drumbeat in the beige.

I told them what I'd told myself: we were partners. She trusted me, approved everything, leaned on me when no one else could. If she denied it, it was only because they frightened her. If she distanced herself, it was only to survive.

One officer scribbled something in his notes when I said that. Scribbling is worse than silence. Silence you can interpret. Scribbling is permanent.

At night, when the lights dimmed, I pressed my forehead to the glass window of the door, staring out at the empty hallway. Sometimes I thought I saw her there, just a flicker, just the shape of her hair in the dim light. She never came closer, never spoke, just lingered at the edge of vision.

I whispered to her through the glass:
"I know you're still with me. You don't have to say it. I'll carry it for us."

The next morning, they handed me papers to sign. Legal disclaimers, acknowledgment of rights, consent for counsel. I signed *Aaron* but, in my mind, I wrote *for us*. Because every signature of mine carried hers, every approval, every keystroke, every whispered *okay*.

The beige walls couldn't erase that. The red camera eye couldn't deny it.

They thought they had locked me away. But really, they had locked *us* together.

And I would never leave her. Not even here.

Chapter 26 – Ghost Letters

Paper is more dangerous than glass.
Glass shows you yourself. Paper lets you rewrite yourself.

They gave me a yellow legal pad and a dull pencil "for notes." I used it for letters. Not to my lawyer. Not to my family. To her.

Lily,

They think you betrayed me. But I know better. You were only protecting yourself, just like I always protected you. When you typed "okay," you said yes forever. You can't take that back. You needed the money for your father's cancer treatment; the bills were crazy you told me.

I filled pages like that, long letters that curved between confession and devotion, guilt and worship. Some read like apologies, others like sermons.

We weren't just colleagues. We were fire. We burned the noise away.
Don't let them convince you you're innocent. Innocent people are powerless. We were powerful together.
You'll read this someday. You'll understand.

Of course, no one would let me send them. The guards collected the pad each night, skimmed for contraband. They never questioned the words, why would they? To them, it was the rambling of a man circling the drain.

But to me, they were proof. Proof that the bond still existed, even if it lived only in graphite.

I tore one page free and pressed it flat against the glass window of the cell door, whispering her name as if she might walk by and see it. The paper fogged where my breath touched, then sagged and slid to the floor.

Ghost letters. Messages trapped in a world of beige and glass.

One night, I wrote a letter that terrified even me:

Lily, if they take me away, you must follow. Because if you stay free, and I am bound, then we are not equal. And we are equal. Always equal. Married through the ledger. Bound through the glass.

I folded that page smaller and smaller, until it was a hard knot in my fist. I didn't hand it in. I tucked it beneath the thin mattress, pressed flat against the steel. My secret vow.

The next morning, when they asked if I had anything to say before the hearing, I almost told them: *Yes. I have letters. Hundreds. Proof that she's still mine.*

Instead, I just smiled. Because some things are too sacred for auditors and lawyers. Some things live only in graphite and whispers.

And she would read them someday.
She had to.

Chapter 27 – The Trial

The courtroom was carved from oak and silence. Every cough, every shuffle of paper seemed amplified, as if the air itself was listening.

And then she walked in.
Lily.

She took the stand with her hands clasped so tightly they shook. The oath was recited, her voice steady but quiet. I watched every syllable, every blink, every tremor. When she said *"I do"* to the oath, I imagined she was saying it to me.

The prosecutor began, his tone crisp and rehearsed.

Prosecutor: "Ms. Bradshaw, can you confirm your role at the bank?"
Lily: "I manage reconciliation for international transfers."
Prosecutor: "And does that role require you to approve adjustments when discrepancies arise?"
Lily: "Yes."
Prosecutor: "Did you rely on Mr. Reid, Aaron Reid, for technical explanations of these

discrepancies?"

Lily: "Yes. He was the subject-matter expert."

The prosecutor advanced a slide on the projector. My annotations glowed in red.

Prosecutor: "Exhibit 14 shows an adjustment of $250,000 routed outside standard treasury channels. Did you approve this?"

Lily: (hesitating) "Yes."

Prosecutor: "At the time of approval, were you aware funds were being diverted to an unauthorized account?"

Lily: "No."

Prosecutor: "So you deny knowledge of wrongdoing?"

Lily: "Yes."

The crack widened. Every *no*, every *deny*, every *yes* spoken in defense of her own innocence felt like a blade turned inward.

The defense attorney rose for cross-examination, his voice softer, coaxing.

Defense: "Ms. Bradshaw, you said you trusted Mr. Reid's expertise?"

Lily: "Yes."

Defense: "So if he told you a discrepancy was routine, you had no reason to doubt him?"

Lily: "That's correct."

Defense: "You relied on him. You believed him?"
Lily: "Yes."

The word *yes* again, but not the way I wanted. Not the way I remembered.

Defense: "Would you say he misled you?"
Lily: (long pause) "He…presented things in ways I didn't question at the time."
Defense: "So you were unaware of any deliberate misconduct?"
Lily: "Yes."

The jury scribbled. The judge nodded. And me? I was drowning.

I wanted to stand and shout: *She knew! She said yes to me in every approval, every late-night message, every silence we shared!* But the shackles on my wrists clinked, cold against my skin, reminding me I had no voice here.

As Lily stepped down from the stand, her eyes never met mine. Not once. She walked past as if I was just another piece of furniture in the courtroom, as if the ledger, the glass, the fire, the need, none of it had ever existed.

And in that absence, the betrayal was complete.

The echoes of Lily's testimony still hung in the air when the lawyers resumed their duel.

The prosecutor rose first, voice sharp as glass. "Ladies and gentlemen of the jury, what you've just heard is the simplest truth: Aaron Reid engineered a system of concealment. He created an unauthorized staging bucket, rerouted funds, and used Ms. Bradshaw's trust as a shield. He exploited her diligence and her fatigue, weaving his crimes beneath her approvals."

Every word was another nail driven into me. *Exploited her trust.* They couldn't see it. I hadn't exploited anything, we had built it together.

The defense countered, his tone smoother, like oil over stone.
"Trust is not a crime. Reliance on expertise is not misconduct. Ms. Bradshaw herself admitted she deferred to Aaron because he was the subject-matter expert. If there was fault, it was systemic. If there was weakness, it was in oversight, not intent."

The jury scribbled again, heads bent. I tried to read their pens, the angle of their brows, the twitch of their mouths. Were they writing *guilty*? Or were they writing *she knew*?

Michelle was called briefly, her voice crisp and certain. "I flagged irregularities. I raised concerns. I was ignored." She cut glances at me like blades. To her, this was vindication.

AJ spoke too, quieter, sadder. "Aaron was one of my best. I trusted him. If these findings are true, I'm...shaken."

Shaken. That word hit harder than guilty. To disappoint a stranger is nothing. To disappoint someone who believed in you? That was a crime deeper than fraud.

Through it all, Lily sat at the side of the room, head down, hands folded. She didn't look at me once. She didn't flinch when the prosecutor painted me as a manipulator. She didn't speak when the defense painted her as a pawn. She just sat there, silent, erasing us with every minute she refused to see me.

When the judge called recess, the jury filed out. They didn't glance at my way. Not even curiosity. To them, I wasn't a man anymore. I was a case file, a string of exhibits.

The bailiff touched my shoulder. Cold metal at my wrists. Chains clinking in silence. I glanced back one last time at Lily.

Her chair was empty.

And that was the betrayal. Not her words, not her denials. The emptiness. The absence.

The fire was gone. Only ash remained.

Chapter 28 – Through the Dark Glass

Prison glass is thicker than courtroom glass. It doesn't just separate. It smothers.

The first time they led me into the visitation room, I saw my reflection in the barrier before I saw the faces on the other side. Pale, cracked, unfamiliar. The glass didn't just reflect, it fractured, scattering me into shards.

No one came to visit. Not AJ. Not Michelle. Certainly not Lily. The seats across from me stayed empty, week after week.

But the emptiness didn't matter. The reflection was enough.

I leaned forward, pressing my palms against the cold pane. The shadow leaned back, mirroring me. It was the only companion left who never betrayed me.

I whispered to it the way I once whispered to her.
"You're still here. You'll always be here."

The guards shifted behind me, restless, but they didn't understand. This wasn't madness. This was faith. Through the dark glass, I could still see her. Not her face, not her body, but the imprint she had left. The ledger of us, written in approvals and silences.

At night, in my cell, I dreamed of keystrokes. Her *okay* echoing like vows through the quiet. I woke with my hands trembling, reaching for a keyboard that wasn't there, a reflection that had already slipped away.

Somewhere beyond these walls, Lily lived free. Denying. Forgetting. Erasing.
But here, through the glass, she was mine. Always mine.

Because glass remembers what flesh denies. Because reflections can't testify.
Because in the end, there is no difference between obsession and eternity.

I closed my eyes, pressed my forehead to the pane, and whispered one final vow:

"You can't erase me. Not here. Not ever."

The shadow nodded back.

And the fire that had long turned to ash smoldered quietly, forever trapped…
through the dark glass.

Part Five: Checkmate

Chapter 29 – Appeal Granted

Freedom was not a miracle. It was paperwork, endless and suffocating.

For months, I had filed motions from my cell. Handwritten appeals, scrawled on yellow pads under the eye of the red camera light. Pages littered with case law, fragments of arguments, and my own whispered annotations: *She knew. She was there. She typed yes.*

The guards thought I was mad, talking to the glass as I pressed my forehead against the cold pane. They didn't understand that the glass was a witness too. Every reflection carried proof. Every shard remembered.

I told the court of appeals what the prosecutors had ignored: Lily wasn't a victim. She wasn't innocent. She wasn't some fragile bystander manipulated by me. She had signed her name, approved the transfers, deferred to my notes too many times and was not incompetent in any way. She had said *okay* and meant it.

The motions piled higher than my meals. Some were returned unread. Some were stamped *DENIED*. But persistence wears down even stone, and obsession sharpens arguments the way fire tempers steel. I wrote until my fingers cramped, until my voice gave out from whispering drafts to my own reflection.

And then, one gray morning, the words came back different:

"Conviction vacated. Prosecution overlooked material co-conspirator. Case remanded for retrial. Witness status revoked."

The court had said it. Out loud.
The obvious truth I had carried alone in the glass was now carved into the record: Lily was not a witness. She was a co-conspirator.

When the gates opened, the clang was not iron but bells. The air outside smelled raw, sharp, almost poisonous after years of beige and disinfectant. But it was freedom. Conditional, suspended, temporary, but freedom all the same.

Reporters swarmed like carrion birds.
"Mr. Reid, do you feel vindicated?"
"Do you blame Ms. Bradshaw?"
"Do you think the retrial will prove your innocence?"

I said nothing. Let them fill the silence with their stories. The only story that mattered was this: I had walked out, and she had been dragged in.

Back in my apartment, dust lay thick on the shelves. The cracked mirror above the sink caught my eye, the fracture branching wider since the day they took me. I touched it and saw my reflection splinter into fragments, each shard another Aaron whispering the same word:

"Lily."

The retrial was not a threat. It was union. The law had finally recognized what I had always known: if I was guilty, so was she. If I was bound, then so was she.

We were together again, in ink and statute, in silence and suspicion.

And now I could wait for her.
Because she would come.
She always came.

Chapter 30 – Return to the Apartment

The apartment smelled of dust and abandonment, but to me it smelled like resurrection.

The locks turned the same way they always had. The hinges creaked the same. The walls, yellowed and cracked, seemed to lean forward to listen as I stepped inside. It was as if the place had been waiting for me.

I ran my fingers over the furniture, over the counters, over the cracked mirror above the sink. The fracture in the glass had spread wider in my absence, jagged lines spidering across the reflection. My face broke into a dozen pieces, each shard watching me with feverish devotion.

I whispered into it.
"She'll come."

For days, I lived on whispers and waiting. No television. No phone. Just the hum of the refrigerator and the tick of the clock. Every sound was her footstep. Every creak in the pipes was her voice. At night, I lay on the couch staring at the ceiling, convinced I could hear the echo of her heels in the hallway outside.

It wasn't paranoia. It was inevitability. Romantic fatalism written in glass. The retrial had tied us together again, and strings always pull taut. She would come, not because she loved me, not because she hated me, but because the glass demanded it.

I left the door unlocked. Always. I wanted her to know she could walk in. That she was expected. That she was already here in everything I touched.

Sometimes I thought I smelled her perfume, faint as smoke, drifting in from the hall. Other times I saw her shadow in the mirror, blurred, just beyond reach.

One night, as I sat in the dark, I felt the certainty coil tight inside me: she was near. Not imagined. Not whispered. Real. The air shifted, heavy and electric.

I turned toward the door and said it aloud, voice shaking with something between longing and dread:
"Lily."

Chapter 31 – The Gun

The door didn't creak when it opened. It whispered, like a breath drawn too sharply in a quiet room.

I had been waiting in the dark, the apartment stripped of sound but alive with anticipation. When the shadow slipped across the threshold, my heart clenched with the inevitability of it.

"Lily," I whispered.

She didn't answer.

She stepped inside with slow, deliberate movements. Sunglasses shielded her eyes though it was well past midnight. A scarf wrapped her throat, hair pulled back tight. She looked less like a visitor, more like a verdict.

And in her hand, she carried it, small, black, heavy with history. I recognized it from stories she'd told in passing once, about her father, a man who had kept an old revolver in a locked drawer. Now it was in her hands, steady, trembling only at the edges.

"You came," I said, rising halfway from the couch, my voice breaking with something that was relief and terror twisted together.

"I shouldn't have," she answered, her voice flat, low.

"You had to. The retrial... they bound us again. They see it now, what I always knew."

She raised the gun. "Stop."

The barrel fixed on me like a black pupil, unblinking.

I laughed, sharply and cracked. "That's not who you are. You couldn't even look me in the eyes in court, and now you're going to kill me?"

Her jaw tightened. The glasses reflected on me back, a broken figure hunched in the dark. I tried to step closer, hands open, pleading.

"I did this for us. Every adjustment, every number, every whisper, I did it for you. Because you were drowning in the bills of your late Dad's cancer treatment. Because you said yes. Because you trusted me."

The silence pressed heavy between us. Only the hum of the refrigerator filled it, low and constant.

Finally, she spoke: "No. You did it for yourself. I never asked you for money and I was too tired to stop you."

The words cut deeper than the gun ever could.

Still, I smiled. Because the glass told me another truth. She was here. She had come. Whether with love or rage, she had come.

And that meant she was still mine.

Chapter 32 – Final Confrontation

The first shot tore through the silence like glass shattering.

It hit my shoulder, spun me against the wall. Heat and numbness spread down my arm, blood blooming through my shirt. I slid to the floor, gasping, staring up at her.

Lily stood steady, gun leveled. Sunglasses still in place. A black mask where her face should have been.

"Lily," I coughed, dragging myself across the floor toward her, each movement leaving a red smear. "Don't... don't walk away now. Not after everything."

"Stay down." Her voice was iron.

But I couldn't. I crawled closer, every inch pulling me through the broken mirror of my own delusion. She had come. She was here. That was all that mattered.

"I did it all for us," I rasped. "The notes, the buckets, the lies, the money. Every number was for you. And you came back. You always come back."

"Stop."

I reached the edge of her shadow. My blood pooled across her shoes. I lifted my hand, trembling, reaching for the glasses.

"Just once," I begged. "Take them off. Let me see your beautiful eyes. One last time. Please."

For a moment, she was still. My reflection wavered in the black lenses, fractured, pathetic, desperate. Then her hand twitched, toward the frame of the glasses. Hope seared me like fire.

But instead of lifting them, she tightened her grip on the gun.

"No," she said.

The second shot was cleaner than the first. Straight to the chest.

The ceiling tilted, the shadows swam. I felt the glass breaking inside me, shards cutting everything to pieces. My breath rasped once, twice.

Her outline hovered above me, faceless, implacable. The gun lowered slowly, but the glasses stayed on. She would not give me her eyes. Yet in this death lies my salvation.

My last whisper bled out with the last of my strength.

"Lily…" The world went dark.

Epilogue – Ashes in the Glass

The newspapers said it plainly: *Disgraced banker shot dead by former colleague.* The reporters used words like "revenge," "rage," "self-defense." They pieced together fragments, her testimony, his release, the retrial looming, but no one could say for certain what had passed in the apartment that night.

Some whispered she had killed him out of anger, unable to bear the weight of his obsession any longer. Others believed she had acted out of fear, cornered by a man who would never stop chasing her reflection.

But there were others, quiet voices who suggested something darker. That Lily had not acted from fear or fury, but from calculation. That she had waited until he was free, until he was vulnerable, until the story could be hers to control. That she had chosen the ending deliberately.

No one could agree. And Lily never explained.

She returned to work in silence, sunglasses hiding her eyes. When asked, she gave nothing away. No confession. No denial. Only silence, like a mirror refusing to reflect.

And so, the question lingers, unanswerable as the cracks in broken glass:

Did Lily kill Aaron because she hated him? Because she loved him still? Because she wanted to save herself?
Or because, at last, she had learned what he always knew,
that through the dark glass, you can rewrite any truth you need to survive?

The glass never says.

It only remembers.

Thank you

Thank you so much for reading. If you enjoyed this book, please leave a 30 second review on Amazon.

Printed in Dunstable, United Kingdom